DROITWICH

THIS BOOK IS DEDICATED
TO LUCA AND WILF

First published in Great Britain in 2014 by Simon and Schuster UK Ltd,
a CBS company.
Simon & Schuster UK Ltd
1st Floor, 222 Gray's Inn Road, London WC1X 8HB

www.simonandschuster.co.uk

Text copyright © Jack Carson 2014
With special thanks to Matt Whyman and Michelle Misra
Cover illustration copyright © Lorenzo Etherington 2014
Interior illustration copyright © Damien Jones 2014

The right of Jack Carson, Lorenzo Etherington and Damien Jones to be identified
as the author and illustrators of this work respectively has been asserted by them
in accordance with sections 77 and 78 of the Copyright,
Designs and Patents Act, 1988.

A CIP catalogue record for this book is available from the British Library.

PB ISBN: 978-0-85707-565-9
eBook ISBN: 978-0-85707-566-6

1 3 5 7 9 10 8 6 4 2

Printed in the UK by CPI Group (UK) Ltd,
Croydon, CR0 4YY

BATTLE CHAMPIONS

TERMINAL TAKEDOWN

JACK CARSON

SIMON AND SCHUSTER

THE CHAMPIONSHIP TRAIL

The Canyon

airie Territory

Mines

Rust Town

dlands

Mines

OCEAN
TERMINAL

Prologue

Sometime in the future, a war destroys the world as we know it. As people struggle to rebuild their lives, a new sport emerges from the ruins. In the Battle Championship, giant robots known as 'mechs' square up to one another and fight like gladiators. They're controlled from the inside by talented pilots, in a fight that tests man and machine to the limit.

All kids grow up dreaming of piloting a mech, and Titch Darwin is no exception. But for Titch it's personal. He is the son of one of the greatest Battle Champions – a man who went missing on the Championship trail – and the only way for Titch to find out what happened is to follow in his father's footsteps . . .

1

On the Trail

Titch Darwin was first to spot the city skyline. It took shape on the horizon, shimmering in a heat haze. Beyond, the sea spread out far and wide.

'There it is,' he called out, pointing at the same time. 'Ocean Terminal. The Championship trail stops here, my friends! Titch was heading for the coast on horseback, alongside his team mechanic, Martha. She looked back to report the news to her twin brother, Finn, but he had already seen the cluster of skyscrapers for himself.

'How could I miss it?' Finn radioed down to her. 'I've got the best seat in the house!'

Titch overheard the message and grinned. He glanced over his shoulder at the giant mech striding behind them. The massive metal robot was part of the team – a Battle Championship contender called LoneStar. Titch raised his gaze to LoneStar's reinforced glass chest plate. He could see Finn in the cockpit, surrounded by panels of switches and dials. He was pushing the control sticks to steer the mech towards the city. It was to be their destination for the weekend.

'Let's hope they're ready for this Battle Championship round,' said Martha. 'Something tells me it's going to be epic!'

•

As a team, Titch, Martha and Finn worked closely together. With her toolkit at hand, Martha made sure that LoneStar was in perfect working order. Finn served as the test pilot. It was his job to report back how the mech was handling, in order to fine-tune the system and make sure it was equipped with the right weapons. Between them, the twins guaranteed that LoneStar was in fighting form. As for Titch, the team's star pilot, he fought in an explosive sport that saw mechs face one another like gladiators.

'What kind of set-up will we need for the battleground here?' asked Titch, who had returned his attention to the city.

'We're heading to the docklands on the far side,' said Martha. 'It was badly bombed during the war, which makes it an ideal venue for this round of the Battle Championship. Unlike the canyons and the swamps where we've fought before, this is a massive stretch of industrial warehouses and concrete wharves overlooking the sea. You'll find supertankers in the water, but they've been scuttled and half sunk. There are also masses of transportation containers. They can offer good cover when you come under fire.'

'Who says we'll come under fire?' joked Finn, using LoneStar's radio system to communicate with his friends. 'Titch has been this season's rising star!'

'Then let's hope we make it there in one piece,' said Martha, looking around.

The trio were careful when they travelled from one battleground to the next with their mech. Each time they set out on the long journey, they risked coming under attack from mech-rustling bandits seeking to steal their machines, break them into valuable parts and sell them at the border. The trail out to the coast had a reputation for being particularly dangerous, so the competing Battle Championship teams had elected to travel in convoy this time.

'You could be in for quite a fight this weekend,' said Finn, who only had to glance at his radar to see that LoneStar was in the middle of a long procession of mechs. He couldn't miss the hulking giant up ahead known as SolarShock. This mech possessed a power system that harnessed the sun's energy. It was mirror-plated from head to foot, and gleamed so brightly that it hurt the three friends just to look at it.

'Let's hope it's overcast if we come to fight that bad boy,' said Finn.

'SolarShock doesn't work like that,' chuckled Martha. 'It has a power unit that stores up huge amounts of energy to see it through all kinds of conditions. I've seen that mech in fighting form even when the sky's been choked up with smoke from the battle.'

Finn sighed wearily. 'Well, maybe we'll strike lucky and fight less dazzling opponents first.'

This time it was Titch's turn to laugh.

'Finn, every mech in this convoy could crush LoneStar in battle if we make a single mistake. Our mech isn't exactly state of the art, but it hasn't let us down yet. Even if it is a little rusty, we're here to win, right?'

'Right!' Riding alongside Titch, Martha raised her hand for a high-five. 'Let's make this a weekend to remember,' she added, encouraging her horse to pick up the pace.

•

The afternoon sun was beginning to sink as they passed through the city gates. Inside the walls, it felt as if every resident had spilled out onto the streets to welcome them. Still in convoy, the mechs and their teams strode along an avenue flanked by towering skyscrapers. The pavements were packed, while ticker tape fluttered down from the rooftops where people craned for a glimpse of their heroes.

'This is incredible,' said Martha, who had to shout to make herself heard over

the din. 'What a welcome!'

'I've never seen anything like it,' agreed Titch. 'How does it look from up there, Finn?'

'Like a dream come true,' came the response. 'Hold on, though. Looks like there's a diversion up ahead.'

Titch stood up in his stirrups for a better look. Sure enough, a group of lawmen were poised to step out into the avenue once SolarShock had passed. Then they began to indicate that the next mech in the convoy should pull right at the next block.

'That's us,' muttered Martha. 'Have we done something wrong?'

'Maybe they just want us all to take different routes to the docks,' Finn suggested, 'so that everyone gets a chance to see a Battle Championship contender?'

Amid the cheering crowds, Titch and Martha pulled up at the next block and followed the directions that the lawmen indicated. Every officer wore dark glasses under a peaked cap. None of them were smiling.

'I hope we're not being pulled over for speeding,' said Titch, though he was only half joking.

As they turned, it struck all three friends that the side street was unusually quiet. There were no crowds. Apart from the lawmen, not a single person was here to watch them pass.

'Something isn't right with this,'

muttered Titch. He glanced behind him. The cops who had steered them away from the avenue had now spanned the street and were following close behind. When one of them quietly unclipped his gun holster, Titch looked ahead once more and pulled up with a start. 'They're not lawmen!' he gasped, as another group of surly-looking figures stepped out of the shadows. Instead of official uniforms, these guys wore tasselled leather trench coats and black ten gallon hats. All of them carried shotguns, but what commanded Titch's attention was the eight-legged mech that crawled into view behind them. He gasped at their appearance, for a spider mech could mean just one thing: the bad guys had also come to town. A moment after it came to a stop, the top hatch spun open and a familiar figure emerged. The man was wearing a racoon-pelt hat and sported a drooping moustache. He also had a

baleful look in his eyes.

'Wyatt Thorne,' Titch breathed, coming face to face with the outlaw who had caused him so much trouble on the Championship trail. 'Wyatt and his Wired Bunch!'

'Well, howdy.' The outlaw spat a wad of chewing tobacco from his mouth. 'I see you've met my partners in crime already.'

Titch glanced over his shoulder. Behind LoneStar, the men he had believed to be lawmen were now peeling off their glasses,

caps and badges. As some shrugged off their police jackets to reveal well-worn shirts and sleeveless leather jerkins, Titch knew full well that he was looking at yet more bandits from Wyatt's gang.

'Finn,' Titch whispered into the radio microphone clipped to the collar of his T-shirt, 'tell me LoneStar is armed!'

'I wish I could,' came the reply, 'but the truth is we're totally exposed.'

Titch glanced at Martha, well aware

that some of the Wired Bunch were beginning to close in on them.

'You're supposed to be behind bars!' Titch called out, still astounded to find himself trapped by his old adversary.

Wyatt Thorne chuckled in response.

'You know what they say,' he told Titch with a shrug. 'The bigger the jail, the better the jailbreak. I always have friends on the outside who can bust me out. This time, all it took was a horse and cart, a length of rope strapped to the bars and – bingo. I'm a free man once again!'

'You won't get away with this!' Titch cried out.

'Well, who's going to stop me?' asked Wyatt? 'There's no point hoping your daddy will come riding in to rescue you because he's dead and buried, right?'

Titch frowned. Once again, the outlaw was toying with his emotions. His father had been a Battle Championship legend.

Many years earlier, he had gone missing while travelling from one battleground to the next. Everyone assumed he had been killed in an ambush by bandits, only Wyatt Thorne continued to tease Titch and leave him questioning whether he might still be alive.

'Now would be a good time to get out of here – and fast!' hissed Martha. 'Whenever Wyatt plays mind games like this, it's always followed by a serious strike!'

Titch looked around. They were closed in on each side by high-sided buildings, with bandits blocking any way to exit the street.

'There's only one thing for it,' said Titch, who watched as Wyatt Thorne lit up a fat cigar.

'What's that?' asked Finn desperately.

'We fight!' he declared, grasping the reins of his horse.

• • •

2

Under Fire

Titch and his two friends were surrounded and outnumbered. In desperation, he peered up and down the street. Titch could think of only one way out of this fix. It was a long shot, but he had become used to taking big risks. Even if it ended in failure, he could at least say that he'd tried his best.

'Finn!' he yelled, as the bandits began to close in. 'Get me into the cockpit!'

Even before he'd drawn breath, a footplate had extended from LoneStar's chest. Then, with a whir of cogs, a series of steel steps slotted out towards the ground.

The first bullet whizzed by as the last step locked into place, startling Titch's horse. It reared up, tossing the boy to the ground, while Martha scrambled to dismount. Together, under a hail of gunfire, they sprinted for the steps. The cockpit was designed for just one pilot. By the time the pair reached the footplate, Finn had evacuated the seat. He knew full well that Titch could bring the mech alive like no other. If the team stood a chance of survival, the smart move was to let the boy take the controls.

'We'll just have to stay low,' Finn yelled at his sister, though Martha didn't need to be told to duck as the bandits continued to fire at them. Even though they were safer on the footplate outside LoneStar's cockpit than on their own at ground level, the pair were still badly exposed. By now, the two horses had galloped to safety. Not a single outlaw paid them any attention. They were here for the three friends and their highly-prized mech.

'Hold tight!' Titch warned, as he strapped himself in and pressed a button to fold the steps away. It left Finn and Martha huddled against LoneStar's body shell for protection. 'Things could get a little bumpy!'

With one hand, Titch swept a row of switches from red to green. LoneStar lurched upright, as if emerging from a slumber. Then a synthesised voice addressed him from a speaker on the console.

'Ready to roll, hot shot!' Hearing the onboard computer immediately set Titch at ease. In every battle he'd faced, they'd worked closely together to get the best out of LoneStar. Right now, as bullets could be heard striking the giant's shell, Titch depended on the computer's sense of calm and logic.

'OK, LoneStar,' he muttered, grasping the control sticks. 'Let's clear this roadblock!'

Titch had already spotted the hydrant

on the pavement beside them. There was one on every block, providing high-pressure water for the fire crews if there was ever a blaze. Just then, faced with a very different sort of fire-fight, Titch steered LoneStar around until the cross hairs on the screen centred on his target.

'What's the plan?' cried Finn through the open cockpit hatch. 'Martha and I daren't even peep over the edge of the footplate. Those bullets are coming thick and fast!'

'The plan is to play a game I've just invented,' replied Titch, through gritted teeth. At the same time, he directed the machine to wrench the hydrant from the ground. At once, a jet of water spat into the air. 'It's called Bandit Bowling!'

In one fluid move, Titch thrust LoneStar onto one knee while swinging the hydrant forward. He released it and watched the pillar tumbling towards the Wired Bunch.

Already drenched in water from the broken mains, the bandits took one look at the incoming hydrant and scrambled from its path. Several slipped, but managed to throw themselves clear, while one shot uselessly at it. With a clang, the hydrant hit the spider mech's front legs and came to a halt. Wyatt peered down at it and shook his head.

'You'll have to bowl better than that for a full strike out,' he said, before dropping back inside his mech. With a groan of metal joints in need of oil, the machine lifted itself onto all eight legs. Then a cannon muzzle extended from the front of the turret and took aim.

'Get into the alleyway!' cried Martha. She gestured desperately at a passage between two buildings. It was cluttered with piles of cardboard boxes and vegetable crates, but looked just wide enough for LoneStar. 'We need cover,

Titch, quickly!'

Titch didn't hesitate. As he passed a balcony overlooking the alley, it allowed his two friends to jump from the mech to safety. Martha vaulted the balcony railings effortlessly. As Finn followed, several of the bandits who had posed as lawmen climbed to their feet and opened fire. It forced Finn to throw himself over the railing, only for his foot to catch as he landed on the other side.

'My ankle!' he cried out, grimacing in pain.

'It's just a sprain!' said Martha, crouching to look, before turning to address Titch once more. He had backed LoneStar into the alleyway. At the entrance, brick dust was popping from the wall with every bullet strike. Martha grabbed the balcony bars and called out to him. 'You'll find a lob bomb in a steel compartment behind the pilot's chair! LoneStar isn't armed, but it's still possible for you to throw it by hand. You'll just have to be quick! It'll explode just seconds after you've activated it!

'But that device is designed to be launched by a mech,' said the onboard computer. 'Surely Titch doesn't possess the strength to throw it far enough in time?'

'There's no way we can climb out to fit it to the launcher,' Martha yelled across. She shrank back for a moment as a bandit opened fire at the balcony. 'If we're going to get out of here in one piece, it's our only chance!'

Titch reached around in his seat. He found the compartment under a fuel gauge. With great effort, he eased the device into his hands. It was the size of a football, with a digital control panel embedded into the casing.

'I need a four-digit code to activate it,' Titch reported, glancing around to see

Wyatt's spider mech creeping into view at the mouth of the alleyway. 'What's the code, Martha?'

'Your birthday,' she told him over the headset. 'Do you need reminding of the date? Hurry, Titch!' As she spoke, yet more bullets slammed against the mech.

'LoneStar,' he said, twisting back in his seat. 'I want you to open up the cockpit hatch for three seconds max. Can you do that for me?'

'Are you sure?' the onboard computer asked. 'The hatch is bulletproof. You're not.'

'I plan to make this throw count,' Titch muttered. 'Our lives depend on it.'

Up ahead, he couldn't ignore the sight of the spider mech's canon taking aim. Immediately, he punched his birthdate digits into the panel of the lob bomb.

'Martha, Finn, take cover behind the balcony railings!' he cried, as the hatch opened before him. Without hesitating,

Titch pushed out onto the footplate and heaved the sphere into the air.

For a moment, it seemed as if every bandit ceased fire to watch as the lob bomb dropped down in front of the spider mech, bounced forward and then rolled to a halt.

'Get back inside, Titch,' the onboard computer commanded. 'Now!'

Coming to his senses, Titch threw himself into the cockpit. As he did so, the sphere cracked open like an egg just moments before it went off. There were no flames, just a wall of noise as every bandit on the ground was knocked backwards by a blast of pressure, as if hit by an invisible wave. Even the windows in the surrounding buildings shattered and imploded, while a ring of debris spread out and settled over everything. It was the spider mech that took the full force, however. From inside his own cockpit, with the hatch back in place in the nick of time, Titch watched the front four legs of the outlaw's machine bend and buckle. With nothing to support it, the spider mech tipped towards him and then crashed to the ground. At the same time, LoneStar swayed and creaked as the blast passed over them. Titch grabbed the controls to keep the machine on its feet, but the alarm system that began to blare told him they had taken some damage.

'It's the gyro-balance,' said the onboard computer. 'We'll be limping until Martha can fix that up.'

'Never mind that now!' Titch zoomed the onboard camera onto the crippled hulk that was once Wyatt Thorn's eight-legged mech. There, with the hatch open and smoke rising from within, the outlaw could be seen spluttering for breath. Titch watched him glare in his direction, and then shake his fist.

'You'll pay for this, boy!' he yelled. 'By the time the weekend is over, you'll wish you'd never joined the Battle Championship!'

● ● ●

3

Fighting Fit

Titch and his friends were the only team to arrive at the Battle Championship venue already looking battle-scarred. It was Finn who eased LoneStar into the Armoury. Here in this secure area, the other competing teams were hard at work preparing their mechs for the weekend's battle rounds. The machines stood in rows, looking like giant metal statues, while the crew members scurried around at ground level.

'The sooner we power down LoneStar, the quicker I can get to work on repairs,' said Martha, riding alongside Titch. It had taken a few minutes to calm their horses after the ambush, as well as several sugar lumps.

'Let's hope it doesn't take too long,' said Titch, as Finn hobbled down the steps that had locked in place from LoneStar's cockpit.

'It's a shame you can't patch me up, too,' he said to his sister. 'Only time and rest is going to heal my twisted ankle, so it's good news that Titch takes over from here.'

'What's the bad news?' asked Martha, who could tell her brother was holding something back.

Finn looked uneasy. Then he cleared his throat and jabbed a thumb at the cockpit.

'The onboard computer is reporting that the blast has also cracked a couple of big seals around the cockpit. It means we're no longer watertight,' he explained. 'That could be a big problem so close to the harbour.'

'Only if we're forced to head into the sea,' said Titch, 'then we'd literally be sunk.'

Martha switched her attention between the two boys.

'Let me worry about repairs,' she told them. 'I'll do my best to make it all right. You two should concentrate on your battle strategy – and that begins by finding out who we're fighting in the first round!'

That night, Titch slept badly. All he could think about was the mech he'd been drawn to face in the first knockout round of the weekend: SharkTooth. On the ground, this mech was slow to move and vulnerable. In the water, the machine transformed into a sleek, amphibious fighting machine that could strike without surfacing. If Titch stood a chance, he thought to himself, he'd have to stick to dry land. He lay in his bed, dwelling on his fight tactics as a storm brewed offshore.

By dawn the next day, Titch was anxious to head out with Finn to see how Martha had progressed. Titch found her sitting on her toolbox in LoneStar's shadow. She was studying a blueprint that made no sense to him. Her face was covered in smears of engine oil. She looked dejected but still smiled bravely when she saw him.

'I hope you've packed your swimming trunks,' she joked. 'This mech can manage in the water now, but not for long. I can't stop all the leaks without replacing the cockpit shell, and we just don't have the parts or the time.'

'How long have I got before it fills up?' asked Titch.

'Not long,' she said reluctantly.

Finn looked worried.

'Each battle round is won by the last mech standing,' he pointed out, 'and sometimes that can take hours!'

Martha looked up at the boys with tears in her eyes. She looked exhausted. 'Well, I've tried my best,' she said.

'Which is all that matters,' Titch reassured her. 'If I have to fight with a leaky mech then so be it. We'd be nowhere in this Championship without you, Martha. You're a mechanic in a million!' He helped Martha to her feet, clapped her on the shoulder and then asked both twins to wish him good luck.

'You're going to need it,' Finn called up to him as he scaled the steps towards LoneStar's cockpit. 'Let's hope the water isn't too cold!'

•

Across at the docks, a sea wall protected the harbour from the ocean. The harbour entrance was wide enough for the supertankers to pass through. Now such ships lay scuppered in the shallows, destroyed like so many things during the war. A curving outcrop of rock formed the other side of the harbour entrance. At the far end, a lighthouse stood defiantly against the crashing waves. Beyond, out in the sea, a small island hosted the city's prison colony. From the docks, it was possible to see that even the inmates had gathered at the bars to their windows so that they could witness the weekend's events. When Titch steered LoneStar out of the Armoury, a huge cheer erupted from the crowds. They had filled the grandstands behind the harbour warehouses, which looked out across the battleground. Many spectators had arrived with T-shirts, caps and flags that sported prints of LoneStar in action. With every Battle Championship round so far, Titch had seen more fans show up to support them and now he was looking at the biggest turnout ever.

'This could turn out to be embarrassing,' he muttered, and pushed the buttons to arm the weapon that they had chosen for this round. 'If we hit the water early, we're going to be in trouble.'

'My advice would be to avoid getting wet altogether,' said the onboard computer. 'Not only is the cockpit likely to take on water in the sea, our opponent is in his natural environment under the surface.'

When SharkTooth appeared, lumbering between two buildings, Titch felt the hairs on the back of his neck begin to prickle. On seeing his opponent, the crowd turned their applause to jeers and booing. The rival mech was strikingly different from so many others. It had a long, sleek torso with a fin at the back and walked on short, retractable struts.

'Be careful, Titch,' came a voice across the intercom. It was Martha. She sounded concerned. 'SharkTooth plays cruel and dirty. You can expect some nasty surprises just as soon as the round begins!'

'I'm ready,' said Titch, strapping himself into the cockpit seat. He grasped the control sticks and then located his opponent on the radar screen as it slunk behind a warehouse. 'Let's go fishing!'

'We are weaponised,' confirmed the onboard computer with a series of beeps. 'Your Harpoon Cannon is loaded. Just don't be trigger-happy. It's attached to a steel cable, which I'll wind in if you hit your target. If you miss, it'll take a moment to reel it back into position.'

'Understood,' said Titch, only to gasp as a piercing, high-pitched tone caused every dial and needle in the cockpit to go into the red. Even the radar flickered and then froze. 'What is that?' he yelled over the din.

'A sonar jammer,' reported the onboard computer as a series of alarms began to ring inside the cockpit. 'Clearly SharkTooth is fitted with a device that blocks every sensor available to me. You'll just have to rely on your eyes and ears, Titch. Use your quick wits!'

The onboard computer had barely finished speaking when the first missile slammed into a gantry just behind LoneStar. It was a near miss and prompted Titch to throw LoneStar into a crouch, just as another missile sliced overhead.

'That one just came around a corner!' yelled Titch. 'What kind of weapon is it?'

'AccuSlams,' replied the onboard computer calmly. 'They're laser-guided rockets designed to hunt you down. All the pilot has to do is lock you on as a target and press the trigger. You've had a narrow escape!'

Titch listened closely, his gaze fixed on a wall of shipping containers ahead. SharkTooth had disappeared behind them and that's where the missiles were coming from. Both had screamed out into the open like attack dogs – and Titch was in no mood to wait around for a third. He spun LoneStar around, seeking some shelter, and that's when the next AccuSlam launched into view. Only it didn't follow the same path as the first two. This one rose up like a rocket from behind the containers, whistling as it flew. Then four more followed at once, fanning out as they

shot into the sky to gasps of surprise from the crowds. Nervously, Titch watched the missiles punch through the low-lying cloud. A moment later, the sound of the rockets cut out.

'What is this? A fireworks display?' he asked out loud.

'Er, negative,' replied the onboard computer, just as the rockets returned to view. 'Looks like they've located their target.'

For a moment, Titch watched in awe as the four missiles swung back through the cloud cover looking very different indeed. Now, a steel fin had sprung from every casing, while the tips had opened up like jaws. As each one whistled towards him from a different direction, Titch instinctively grasped the control sticks and hurled LoneStar into action.

'Which way?' he asked.

'That's your call,' the onboard

computer reminded him. 'SharkTooth still has us under sonar blackout!'

With the sound of the incoming missiles building, Titch pushed LoneStar into a sprint. The mech thundered along the length of the dock, past boatyards and the customs house. The crowds in the stands rose to their feet as LoneStar crunched by, but Titch had no opportunity to salute them. Instead, his eyes locked onto a shadow as it began to build just ahead. It looked like an ink drop that slowly spread in size. Titch looked up through the cockpit hatch and gasped.

'Here comes the first missile!' cried Titch. 'We need to take evasive action!'

● ● ●

4
Survival of the Fittest

With no time to lose, Titch slammed the control sticks to one side. In response, LoneStar moved like a rugby player dodging a tackle. The missile hit the ground with an almighty explosion. It knocked the mech off its feet, but only for a moment because Titch detected yet another shadow spreading over them.

'There are three more strikes incoming!' said the onboard computer.

'That's better than four,' grumbled Titch, once more changing direction to distance LoneStar from the growing shadow. This time, he turned from the harbour and sprinted along a quay. A rusting supertanker was moored in the water up ahead. Spotting the anchor chain, Titch threw LoneStar towards it. Stretching the mech's arms outwards, he grabbed a steel link just as the missile detonated behind him. It was a narrow miss, but not for the supertanker. With the hull breached, water could be heard rushing into the hold. On deck, Titch hauled LoneStar onto the deck and looked up. To his surprise, the last two missiles could be seen skimming over the water out to sea.

'What's going on?' he asked, well aware that the ship beneath his feet was beginning to sink into the water. 'Where's SharkTooth?'

'It isn't over yet,' warned the onboard computer, who had started rebooting several drive systems inside LoneStar. 'Give me another ten seconds and I'll get the radar back on. Until then, keep your eyes on those missiles.'

By now, all he could see were tiny

pinpricks on the horizon. But, instead of vanishing, both spread apart for a moment, before coming together and then growing in size once again.

'They've switched back around,' said Titch. 'They're coming right for us!'

'In five seconds' time our systems will be restored!' said the onboard computer. 'And that includes our weapons!'

'But they're no use right now!' said Titch, as the missiles raced low over the water towards them. 'We're sitting ducks here,' he added, looking around for a means of escape. 'OK, there's only one thing for it.'

'What's that?' asked the onboard computer, just as the cockpit alarm stopped ringing and a series of lights indicated that the sonar was no longer jamming the system.

'You're not going to like this,' said Titch, and prepared to take action as the missiles screamed into the harbour, 'but it's time we went for a swim!'

The onboard computer protested immediately, but Titch had made up his mind. The missiles were seconds away, coming in so low that they kicked up a churn on the water's surface before lifting suddenly and twisting into the bridge of the supertanker. The explosion was huge. Titch could feel the blast hit the back of LoneStar as he dived for the water, but it was under the surface before the fireball consumed them. For a moment, all he could see through the murk was the bed of the harbour, some weeds and an anchor. Then something slid through the water up ahead. Something big, bold and menacing. As soon as Titch caught sight of the chrome fin, he identified it straight away.

'SharkTooth!' he declared, fighting with the controls to raise LoneStar onto its feet. 'We're in his territory now!'

All of a sudden, Titch felt out of his depth in more ways than one. Not only could SharkTooth move much faster in the sea, LoneStar was now taking on water through the broken seals of the cockpit hatch. It was pouring in and pooling at his feet.

'Our circuits could short out at any time,' warned the onboard computer. 'And if it rises, you could drown!'

'Thanks for reminding me,' said Titch

bitterly, who was still wrestling with the controls. 'Now do me a favour and focus on pinpointing SharkTooth!'

'Understood.'

Positioning LoneStar onto its feet, and with water still gushing through the lower half of the hatch, Titch found the trigger button and peered through the glass.

'I don't like this,' he muttered as the water swilled around his seat.

'Use the radar, Titch. We're back online!'

Titch glanced at the screen. A moment later, a red light indicated SharkTooth's position. It was moving at speed around the harbour, while the green light showing LoneStar's position remained stationary.

'Sharks circle their prey,' Titch pointed out. 'If we stay here, we're doomed. It's time the hunted became the hunter!'

He moved LoneStar through the water, wading desperately as a glinting metal fin appeared some distance away and began to move around them. All across the harbour, the crowds in the stands were on their feet, while the bombed supertanker had become a blaze. Titch pushed towards a refuelling bay that jutted out into the water.

His plan was to take cover between the iron struts that supported the fuel tank, but SharkTooth was moving so much faster. Titch looked around to check his opponent's position, only to find the fin had disappeared.

'Watch out!' cried the onboard computer, just as Titch checked the radar and saw the red circle was almost upon them.

Titch wheeled LoneStar around, only for his opponent to leap from the water and sail right over them. At the same time, it delivered a solid punch to LoneStar's head, knocking the mech off its feet. With alarm bells ringing, and water sloshing from one side of the cockpit to the other, Titch fought to recover. He caught sight of SharkTooth racing away underwater and felt this battle round slipping away from them.

'Another hit like that and we're finished,' he said, taking aim with the Harpoon Cannon. 'Let's make this count.'

Without further word, Titch unleashed the weapon. The harpoon sped after its quarry, unspooling a steel cord as it darted through the water. Titch watched on the radar as the harpoon caught up, only for SharkTooth to flick it away with its tail.

'You'll have to do better than that!' said the onboard computer. 'Now get some cover while I reel it back in. Until then, we're defenceless!'

Titch didn't hesitate to follow orders. With his sights set on the jetty, and the water inside the cockpit at his waist, he pushed across the harbour as fast as LoneStar could go. Once again, SharkTooth was preparing for another strike. Titch could see the harpoon being dragged back by the winch, but he doubted it would be locked and loaded in time. This time, however, when SharkTooth launched from the water, Titch responded by swiping a punch at the other mech first. It caused SharkTooth to somersault overhead and splash into the shallows, but before Titch could follow up the blow it had swam away.

'It's too fast!' he cried. 'We can't compete in open water!'

For once, the onboard computer made no suggestions. Instead, it finished reloading the Harpoon Cannon and confirmed it was primed to fire. Titch was already pushing LoneStar towards the refuelling bay. All he needed was enough time for him to get underneath the struts before SharkTooth staged his next strike . . .

But then he had an idea. Rather than hiding, maybe he could lure his opponent into a trap? The thought persuaded Titch to push as hard as possible for the refuelling bay. He raced between the struts, well aware that the radar showed SharkTooth had just fallen in behind. But instead of using the struts for cover, Titch weaved his mech through to the other side. He then waded out as fast as he could before turning to fire the Harpoon Cannon. He didn't aim at his rival, however, but at the fuel tank above. It exploded as soon as the harpoon skewered the side, engulfing SharkTooth in flaming fuel and falling girders. The blast knocked LoneStar backwards, but Titch managed to keep the mech upright.

'A knockout move!' crowed the onboard computer as the crowd could be heard roaring their approval from the grandstands. 'Congratulations!'

'We have to make sure the pilot is OK!' said Titch, concerned that his opponent's mech was submerged beneath the burning, mangled heap in front of him. 'Switch to an open communication channel. Let's try and reach him!'

As soon as the onboard computer changed the radio frequency, Titch could hear several members of the fire and rescue crews on the airwaves. They were calling out to the pilot, asking to confirm his status. Titch wasted no opportunity to join them.

'Say something, buddy!' he cried out, attempting to move LoneStar closer to the blaze. 'We're going to get you out of this!'

In a bid to drain the cockpit of water, Titch kicked open the cockpit hatch. At once, he could feel the heat from the blaze. He circled the burning wreckage of the refuelling station. Any elation he had experienced on winning the round had now turned to concern.

'This is bad,' said the onboard computer, who ran through several radar scans in a bid to see through the twisted metal.

'Wait! What's that?' Titch pointed at a dark shape under the water, just pushing out from under the wreckage. 'SharkTooth!'

'I'm OK,' croaked a voice across the airwaves. 'My mech has taken a beating, but I'm safe. Congratulations, Titch. You won fair and square!'

Titch yelled out in relief and delight, punching the air at the same time. Through the hatch, he watched as the pilot disengaged his cockpit from the stricken, sunken mech, which then floated to the surface like a big bubble.

'You had us worried!' he said, as the cockpit bobbed up and down across the water from them, only for another voice to cut across him. This one was on a stronger broadcast channel and addressed Titch's opponent directly.

'You did well to save SharkTooth from being burned to a crisp there. Set the mech in safe mode and sit tight. The rescue boat is on its way.'

The man on the airwaves may have been addressing the other pilot, but Titch didn't breathe. Ignoring the thunder of cheering and applause from the crowd, he just sat there stunned at what he had heard.

'I recognise that voice,' he said after a moment, and sat back in his seat. 'I swear that's my father!'

5
Out of Bounds

Back on dry land, Titch climbed out of his mech to a roar of applause from the crowds. He waved as he hurried down the steps, but when Marsha and Finn met him at ground level, Titch's first-round victory was the last thing on his mind.

'I think my dad's alive!' he said, rushing to tell them what he'd heard over the airwaves. 'He's here! At the docklands!'

The twins glanced at one another warily.

'I know you miss him,' said Martha quietly, 'but Titch, eventually you'll have to accept that he's dead and gone.'

'No way!' cried Titch. 'I heard him!'

Finn looked uneasy. 'Martha is right,'

he said. 'This is all because Wyatt Thorne's given you false hope! He knows you're on the Championship trail hoping to find out what happened to your dad. He's just playing with your mind.'

'But I definitely recognised the voice!' Titch insisted. 'It was my dad, without a shadow of a doubt!'

Just then, SharkTooth's pilot arrived at the jetty on board the rescue boat. He was wearing a life jacket and looked thoroughly dejected. 'Congratulations, Titch,' he said, shaking the boy's hand. 'That was an impressive performance. You're a natural.'

'I need to talk to you,' Titch said quickly, helping him ashore. 'That man who spoke to you on the radio. Who was he?'

The pilot lifted his life jacket over his shoulders and shrugged.

'The transmission came from the control room,' he said. 'I guess it was one

of the officials.'

'Where do I find that room?' Titch sounded desperate.

Raising his palms, the pilot urged Titch to calm down.

'It's behind the Armoury,' he said. 'Inside old harbour master's office.'

Titch didn't reply. He had already sprinted away, hoping desperately to find the man who had disappeared when he was just a little kid. Having apologised to the pilot for their friend's haste, Martha and Finn hurried to catch up. When they found Titch, he had stopped at the oak doors to a dark stone building. A sign outside forbade all Battle Championship contenders from proceeding further.

'This is where the organisers discuss player conduct, rules and regulations,' hissed Martha, keeping her voice down in case someone heard them. 'It's not for your ears, Titch. Only top officials are allowed inside. If you step over that threshold they'll throw you out of the tournament!'

Titch looked torn.

'But if my dad was behind that radio transmission,' he told them, 'then he has to be inside. I can't just walk away now. It's the only reason I'm on the Championship trail!'

Finn stepped back and scanned the building. The blinds were closed inside every window. It didn't look at all inviting.

'I have a bad feeling about this,' he said, shaking his head. 'Come on, Titch. Why don't we bring LoneStar back into the Armoury and celebrate your first-round victory?'

Titch considered Finn's suggestion.

'It's a good idea,' he said, 'but I can't just walk away now.'

'You'll be stopped as soon as you open that door,' said Martha.

'I know,' said Titch. 'That's why I plan

on finding another way in!'

•

Sometimes, being short and slight had its advantages. Titch reminded himself of this when he found a small open window on the side of the building. Squeezing through it, he dropped into a storage room, crouched low and listened. He could hear muffled voices from the floor above. On tip-toes, Titch made his way towards the door.

Opening it just a crack, he saw a guard pacing the lobby. Behind him, a sweeping oak staircase led to the next level. Titch looked behind him, searching for a means to distract the guard. The storage room contained shelves full of stationery. He pulled out a pencil, returned to the door and tossed it into the far corner of the lobby. As soon as it clattered onto the tiles, drawing the guard to investigate, Titch dashed into the open and raced up the stairs.

Keeping low, he could hear the voices much more clearly now. A meeting seemed to be taking place behind the main door on this floor. Titch pressed his ear to the wall and listened. At first, it sounded like a boring discussion around a table about the number of mechs permitted to fight over one weekend. But then someone asked a question about a prototype mech. Titch thought he recognised the voice of the man who answered straight away. It was the same one he had heard earlier – without a doubt, he could hear his father!

'Your engineers have worked hard on perfecting this model,' Titch heard him say. 'Everything is working as expected, but it would be irresponsible to test it here at the Battle Championship. The mech is designed to fight in a war, not a sport.'

'He's right,' said another voice, which again seemed familiar to Titch. 'It's a killing machine!'

'I've heard enough!' replied another man. Titch hadn't heard him before, but he sounded older, gruff and unfriendly. 'The mech will enter the battleground this weekend, whether you like it or not! I will hear no more protests from either of you. This meeting is over!'

Titch caught his breath. He didn't like the sound of what he'd just heard one bit. Nor did he feel comfortable with the

sound of chairs being scraped backwards and footsteps marching towards the door. Before he'd had a chance to hide, the door crashed open to reveal a figure he could not mistake. The man recognised Titch straight away, but it wasn't his father. The last time Titch had seen this figure with the shoestring tie and the ten-gallon hat, he'd been a rookie pilot back at Mech Academy.

'Marshal Johnson!' he said in a whisper.

A look of shock crossed the marshal's face. It quickly turned to concern. He glanced over his shoulder, aware that others were following him to the door, and then glared at Titch.

'You shouldn't be here,' he hissed. 'Get away before someone sees you!'

Titch didn't move, however. Instead, he stood his ground.

'My dad is in there, isn't he?'

Just then, the next official to leave the room appeared behind the marshal's shoulder.

'Who is this boy?' he asked out loud. It was the man who'd just refused to listen to his father's warnings about entering a military mech into the Battle Championship. 'Guards! Arrest this kid for trespassing!'

'Run!' hissed Marshal Johnson, deliberately blocking the door. 'Run for your life!'

This time, Titch didn't hesitate to act on the marshal's order. He had done it countless times at Mech Academy. Spinning around, he hurtled towards the stairs once more, well aware that the guard in the lobby had been drawn by the disturbance. Titch watched him spread his arms wide, blocking his exit. Midway down the steps he glanced up and around.

Spotting the chandelier above the guard's head, dangling from a chain, he launched himself towards it. The guard looked on aghast, reaching up just a moment too late to stop Titch from grasping the chain and swinging over his head.

'Stop him!' yelled a voice from the top of the steps.

Leaping to the floor, Titch glanced around to see yet more officials spilling from the room. He spotted Marshal Johnson looking on with concern in his eyes. Desperate to avoid being recognised by anyone who might expel him from the Championship, and with no time to see if his dad was among them, Titch turned and raced for the main door.

'Excuse me!' he yelled, on crashing out into the sunshine and barrelling through a group of spectators. 'I'm in a rush!'

Having found a gap, Titch promptly crashed into a familiar face.

'Alexei!' he declared, instantly recognising his rival and fellow student from the Academy.

'Hey, have you seen my wallet?' asked the boy, whose blond hair and blue eyes were now familiar to Battle Championship fans across the country. He hadn't noticed that Titch was in a hurry to get away. 'It was in my pocket a moment ago and now it's gone.'

Titch glanced over his shoulder. 'You have to help,' he pleaded. 'Any second now, some security guards are going to spill out of that building looking for me. It's vital that you point them in a different direction,' he added, panting heavily. 'If I'm caught they'll kick me out of the competition!'

Alexei looked at the main door and then back at Titch.

'Why should I help a fellow competitor?' he asked with a sneer. 'One less mech pilot sounds good to me. Especially if it's you!'

Titch grasped his old adversary by the collar. 'Please, Alexei. I'm begging you.'

This time, Alexei couldn't ignore Titch's air of desperation. He glanced at the door once more and nodded.

'You can hide yourself behind some bins back there,' he said, jabbing a thumb over his shoulder. 'But you owe me now!'

● ● ●

6

Submerged!

'Yuk!' Martha looked up from her toolkit and pinched her nose. 'What is that dreadful smell?'

'It's me, I'm afraid,' said Titch, trudging towards her. After his close shave with the guards, he had headed straight for the Armoury, trying hard not to make eye contact with anyone. This had been difficult, because lots of people had looked at him as he passed by and crinkled their faces in disgust.

'What happened to you?' asked Finn, climbing down from LoneStar's cockpit. He approached Titch, looking puzzled and then amused. 'Is that a fish head in your hair?'

Titch removed the offending item. He

tossed it to one side and nodded glumly. Martha kept her distance. She had already seen that he was in fact covered in the oily remains of a very big catch.

'I had to make a hasty exit from the official's building,' he explained. 'Diving into a bin stopped me from being spotted, but I didn't realise it was full of fish guts until it was too late.'

'You need a shower, my friend,' said Finn. 'Even LoneStar won't thank you if you climb into the cockpit without a wash and scrub up.'

Martha laughed, unlike Titch, who just seemed distracted.

'You were wrong about my father,' he said. 'He's here without a shadow of a doubt.'

Finn tipped his head. He looked concerned.

'Your dad's been missing for years,' he said, as if to remind Titch. 'It's understandable that you'd want to believe that he's still with us.'

'Oh, he's with us,' Titch said, and looked Finn directly in the eyes. 'I just don't like the feeling that he's mixed up in something bad.'

•

Titch found it hard to sleep that night. Every time he closed his eyes, his thoughts drifted back to that moment outside the meeting room when he'd felt sure he could hear his father. What he'd had to say troubled the boy. Could there really be a mech in the competition this weekend running a secret trial as a war-fighting machine? If so, thought Titch, that wouldn't just give it an unfair advantage. It would be a killing machine! Then there was his encounter with Marshal Johnson. Back at the Academy, he had taught Titch everything when it came to piloting a mech. But seeing him here at the Battle Championship had come as a complete surprise.

'I will get to the bottom of this,' he told himself. 'Even if it kills me.'

Titch settled down for a moment, only to sit up with a start when something crashed through the window pane. Snapping bolt upright, he caught sight of the metal sphere as it rolled across the floorboards. With a gasp, he recognised it immediately. A lob bomb!

Well-aware that the device was fitted with a short countdown to detonation, Titch hurled himself from the bed, dragging the mattress over him. He bunched up, his eyes squeezed tight, and braced himself for the pressure blast.

Ten seconds later, he dared to open one eye and then the other. He peeked out from under the mattress and frowned. The lob bomb hadn't exploded. It was just sitting there in the middle of his room while a sea breeze blew in through the broken window. Titch knew that when a lob bomb was primed to go off it displayed a digital readout, but this one was dead. He dared to crawl out and then pick it up. As soon as he felt how light it was, Titch realised he was looking at the shell only. He cracked it open, and found a note inside. It read, simply: STAY AWAY.

•

The next day, Titch decided not to share what had happened with Martha and Finn. He also opted not to let them know that he had come face to face with Marshal Johnson. The twins had clearly doubted his claim that his father was here. If he told them he had run into their tutor from Mech Academy they might worry that he was losing his mind. Just then, the last thing Titch wanted to do was take their minds off the task at hand. As a team, it was important that they focused on making sure LoneStar was completely prepared for the second knockout round of the weekend. Even so, when Titch steered the mech out of the Armoury, between crush barriers that held back the crowds, he felt unsettled.

'Something on your mind?' asked the onboard computer. 'My seat sensors tell me you're struggling to get comfortable.'

Titch smiled to himself and piloted LoneStar out onto the dock. Already the sun had risen high into the sky, as if steering a path through majestic clouds.

'Don't worry about me,' he said. 'Let's just throw everything we have into this battle. I'm not going to be scared away from this Championship!'

As he spoke, a dot flashed up on his radar that he hadn't expected to see.

'The system is programmed to detect any threats – and not just inside the battleground,' said the onboard computer. 'It's picked up on the presence of someone who has previously attempted to attack us. There, beside the grandstand, to your right.'

Titch looked around. His opponent had yet to appear, but this still came as a distraction. He peered through the cockpit hatch. A group of people were crowded around a man on a soapbox with a blackboard behind him. They were holding out cash, which he was taking in exchange for slips of paper.

'Those guys are placing bets on the battle,' said Titch. 'I wonder who is favourite to win?'

'Never mind that,' said the onboard computer. 'Take a close look at the man with all that cash in his hand.'

As if to help Titch, the monitor beside the radar zoomed in on the scene. Titch recognised the man's racoon-pelt hat and leather greatcoat immediately, and couldn't ignore the wad of notes in his hand.

'So, Wyatt Thorne is still in town,' he

muttered. 'And with a lot of money to burn.'

Titch half wondered if the outlaw was responsible for throwing the dummy lob bomb into his room. Still, now was not the time to investigate. Not when a mech stepped out onto the wharf like some gunslinger preparing for a shoot-out. Titch recognised the machine straight away. As every beam of sunshine seemed to bounce off its body shell, Titch was forced to shield his eyes.

'Say hello again to SolarShock,' said the onboard computer, and darkened the smart glass inside the cockpit hatch. 'You know what they say about the dangers of staring at the sun? Well, the same thing applies with this mech.'

'What weapons are we facing?' asked Titch, switching the monitor to a satellite map of the battleground.

'SolarShock's team have bolted on a FlareSlayer,' said the onboard computer. 'It fires a white-hot bolt of electricity that could slice through our armour like a knife through butter.'

'OK, so what do we have to hit back?' Titch checked his own weapon system. Martha had fitted LoneStar with an OctoPunch. Finn had been impressed with it in testing, but Titch had yet to try it out for himself. The device, bolted to the mech's wrist, fired eight steel tentacles that each locked onto the same target.

One wasn't enough to floor their opponent, but a repeat strike could easily entangle the machine and bring it crashing to the ground.

'SolarShock has just made the first move,' said the onboard computer. 'It's sprinting out towards the loading bay!'

Titch squinted through the cockpit hatch. Even with the tint raised to maximum, the glare was so intense it was hard to keep SolarShock in his sights. All he could see was a blinding light moving swiftly across the dock. At the same time, what looked like a fork of lightning spat towards LoneStar.

'Hold tight!' cried Titch, throwing the mech to one side, 'we have a big fight on our hands!'

•

Just as Titch had predicted, the battle was long and hard. He found it was just impossible to lock the target on SolarStrike because of the glare. Every time he attempted to take aim, the light proved too intense.

'You'll just have to rely on the radar,' suggested the onboard computer. 'And think ahead!'

Before he'd even had a chance to glance at the screen, LoneStar was knocked to the ground as if hit by a steam train.

'What was that?' cried Titch, amid the howl of system damage alarms.

Hauling LoneStar upright, Titch caught sight of what had just floored them. SolarShock had wrenched the arm of a crane from its fixings and was using it as a club. The rival mech swung it ferociously at LoneStar, forcing Titch to duck and shrink away from swipe after swipe. At the same time, faced with the full glare from SolarShock's mirror skin, Titch found himself struggling to mount a counter-offensive.

'We're running out of wharf!' warned the onboard computer, but by then it was too late. Titch took another step backwards, only for LoneStar to topple backwards into the dock. 'OK, we're all out of wharf!'

With the mech on its back in the water, which rushed across the cockpit hatch and then poured through the cracked seal once more, Titch saw SolarShock peering down at him. With his finger on the trigger, he fired the OctoPunch into the air. Or at least he tried.

'Nothing's happening!' he cried, panicking as he jabbed at the trigger repeatedly.

'The entire system has crashed,' replied the onboard computer, 'and weirdly I can't reboot it!'

Titch squinted up through the water. On the dockside, his opponent took aim with the FlareSlayer. It looked like some kind of trident, except this one was crackling with electricity. All at once, SolarStrike raised the weapon high in one hand and aimed the tip at LoneStar. In a blink, a shard of lightning spat towards the stricken mech. Titch felt a huge jolt as his machine was engulfed in an electric current.

'Is everything OK? he asked the onboard computer. 'Speak to me! Are we still functioning?'

A moment later, as LoneStar began to sink towards the bed of the dock, Titch realised that even the system alarms had fallen silent. It left him all out of options.

With water filling the cockpit, he unstrapped his harness, reached for the override switch to open the hatch and prepared to swim to the surface.

'Are you hurt?' asked Finn, who had been held back by the stewards while the rescue team helped Titch from the water.

'I'm fine,' said Titch, 'but I can't say

the same for LoneStar.'

Martha was standing alongside her brother. She was peering down at the water and the sorry outline of their mech on the harbour bed.

'There are enough cranes here to salvage it,' she said, with a glance at the buckled remains of the one that SolarShock had used to batter LoneStar. 'He totally beat you there, Titch.'

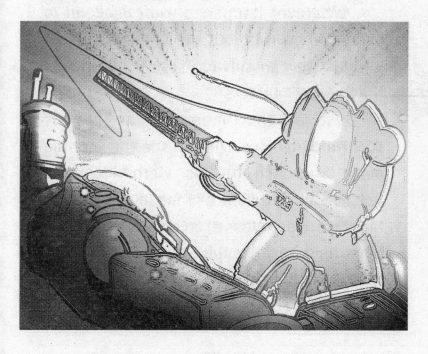

'We were powerless,' Titch protested, shaking the water from his ears. 'As soon as LoneStar hit the water, the system just shut down.'

Martha looked puzzled. 'That shouldn't have happened,' she said. 'It's one thing for the pilot to get drenched inside a leaky cockpit, but the power drive is a sealed unit. LoneStar should've stayed functioning, even with wet feet.'

'Whatever happened, our weekend is over.' Titch wrung out his T-shirt. 'Still, as long as we can salvage LoneStar, I guess that's what matters.'

Just at that moment, the crowds surrounding him turned to see the winning mech approach on his victory parade. SolarShock had a lot of fans in the stands. Most wore sunglasses to counter the glare from its mirror panels, and rose to their feet as he lumbered towards them.

'You tried your best,' said Finn, as he

placed an arm on Titch's shoulder. 'We can't ask for anything more.'

Titch didn't respond. Instead, his attention was locked on the walkway in front of the grandstand. There, a man with a racoon-pelt hat, leather greatcoat and drooping moustache was striding away from the betting stand. The outlaw Wyatt Thorne had a fan of cash in one hand, which he was counting eagerly.

'Looks like someone's hit the jackpot,' observed Martha.

'No doubt by betting that we would lose.'

As Titch sighed and shook his head, a figure passed behind the outlaw that seized his attention.

'Dad?' he called out, and broke away from his friends. 'Dad!'

'No, Titch! Wait!' cried Martha, who had seen what was coming. 'Watch out!'

7

The Chase

Paying no attention to his friends, Titch dashed into the open.

'It's me!' he called out to the figure he felt sure was his father. He noticed that a scar zigzagged down the man's face, which made it hard for Titch to be certain, but then years had passed since they'd last been together. So much could've happened to him in that time. 'Dad! It's me! Your son!'

This time the man glanced across. As soon as Titch met his clear blue eyes, it felt as if he was looking into a mirror. Then the man glanced upwards, just as a huge shadow fell across Titch. He spun around and gasped at the sight of the approaching mech. SolarShock looked even more forbidding from ground level. As its foot came down, Titch threw himself to one side. He felt the ground beneath him shake as the rival mech moved on, clearly unaware of the small boy who had narrowly avoided being crushed. Breathlessly, Titch clambered to his feet but the man on the other side of the dock had disappeared. Instead, he spotted Wyatt Thorne watching him from the crowds. The outlaw was still clutching the money and looked most amused.

'This weekend really isn't working out for you, Titch,' he called across. 'Take my advice and head for the hills. That's if you know what's good for you!'

Ignoring the bandit, Titch scoured the walkway. His eyes flitted from one figure in the crowd to the next, until he spotted the man. With his back turned, walking briskly towards the Scavenger Store, it was impossible for Titch to tell whether or not it was his father. Determined to find out, he broke into a sprint.

'Dad! It's me!' he called out, but the plea was lost under the chattering crowd Please wait!'

The walkway was still packed with people. Titch wrestled his way through. By the time he was clear, the figure he'd been chasing was nowhere to be seen. Wyatt was still watching him. He pocketed his winnings and chuckled.

'So, is he dead or alive, boy? You decide!'

Titch glared at the outlaw.

'This isn't a game!' he cried. 'This is my life you're playing with!' Then, in desperation, he raced off to track his father down.

•

When Titch showed up back at the Armoury, the sun was close to setting.

'Where have you been?' asked Martha.

She was standing behind LoneStar, with a laptop plugged into a socket in the machine's Achilles heel. 'It's a good job we're not fighting another battle round again this weekend,' she added. 'I've tried everything to revive the computer, with no luck. It's completely locked. All I can do is wipe LoneStar's hard drive and reboot the system from scratch.'

Titch nodded. He looked worn out.

'That man I followed was definitely my dad,' he told Martha, which drew her attention. 'I swear it's him!'

'I caught sight of him myself when you dashed in front of SolarShock,' she said. 'You never told me his face was scarred.'

'It wasn't,' said Titch. 'But my dad was a fighter! He proved it in the Battle Championship. If it's true that he was ambushed on the trail, and somehow survived, then I have no doubt that he would've picked up some wounds along the way.'

'So why didn't he respond when you called out to him?'

Titch shrugged. It was a question he just couldn't answer. He wanted to believe that the man had just failed to hear him calling out, but that didn't explain why it felt like he'd been trying to give him the slip. Titch felt hot tears pricking his eyes and blinked them away.

'I've searched all over the docks,' he told Martha, turning his back to her to hide his face. 'I know he's alive. I know he's here. All I need to do now is prove it!'

All around, competing teams were carrying out changes and repairs to their mechs. Some of the machines were in a bad state and had clearly lost their battle rounds. One mech was little more than a twisted heap of metal and burned-out pistons. Its crew were standing before the wreckage, shaking their heads. Titch

spotted SolarStrike further back. The mech's mirrored bodywork looked like it needed a polish after its fight against LoneStar, but nobody was working on it.

'The team have been called to a stewards' review meeting,' Martha explained. 'They were looking for you, too, but Finn volunteered to take your place.'

'What was the problem?' Titch knew that a review only took place if something didn't add up during the knockout round. 'SolarStrike beat me fair and square.'

'I'm not so sure about that!'

Hearing Finn, the pair turned. He dashed towards them, beaming broadly.

'What's up?' asked Titch.

'I've just come from a Championship Enquiry into the last round. There's a reason why LoneStar's system froze,' he told them. 'The pilot was carrying a Mech System Disrupter inside his cockpit. As soon as he set it to transmit, LoneStar was as good as dead.'

'But that's illegal,' said Martha. 'It's also highly dangerous. Titch could've been scaling a building when he switched that on.'

'Do you want to know the best bit?' Finn continued. 'The pilot confessed that he was paid to do it. He claims that he was offered too much cash to turn it down. Said he had a family to support back home. He's been thrown out of the Championship, of course, but guess who put him up to it?'

'Go on,' said Martha, standing now.

As if in response, the sound of angry shouting struck up from the security gates. The three friends, like everyone else around them, turned to see several lawmen hauling a man in handcuffs towards the dockside. A small motor launch awaited them, along with several prison guards.

'Wyatt Thorne!' Titch shouldn't have been surprised. Even so, he was shocked to learn that they had lost their second round through foul play. 'Can you never play by the rules?' he cried out.

'Sure I can,' snarled Wyatt, as the lawmen escorted him under LoneStar's shadow. 'My rules!'

'Not any more,' growled one of the lawmen. 'There's a nice prison cell awaiting you on the island, Wyatt. While you await

trial there, you can play by our rules!'

Wyatt glared at Titch as they passed, struggling to free himself. In the scuffle, a wallet dropped from his pocket.

'I think that belongs to a friend of ours,' said Titch, scooping it up before Wyatt could kick it away. 'So, you robbed Alexei and used the money to swing the battle round? That's a low blow even for you!'

'Oh, I'm full of surprises,' Wyatt said with a sneer. 'And the best has yet to come!'

Titch glanced at his two friends as the outlaw was led away. He felt a little rattled.

'I think he's talking about my dad,' he said.

'Ignore him,' Finn replied. 'Titch, it's important that you stay focused for the rest of the weekend.'

'Why?' asked Titch, toying with Alexei's wallet. 'Our weekend is all washed up now.'

Finn glanced at Martha, who grinned as she worked it out for herself.

'It isn't washed up. It's only just begun!' she cried. 'We're back in the championship! If SolarShock has been disqualified for cheating it means the victory will be handed to us. We're through to tomorrow's final round!'

Titch looked happy, but subdued.

'I thought you'd be thrilled!' said Finn.

'Oh, it's brilliant news,' agreed Titch.

'But it would be even better if I could just get to the bottom of what's going on with my father.'

•

Battle Championship weekends were always busy for the teams. The event at Ocean Terminal was no exception. LoneStar had been hoisted from the bed of the dock thoroughly waterlogged. Yet again, Martha was forced to work late into the night to repair and reprogramme their mech. This time, with victory in sight, she was helped by both her teammates. As a result, the three friends snatched just a couple of hours' sleep before meeting up at dawn once more in LoneStar's shadow.

'I'm so tired!' Finn yawned and stretched. 'Titch, how can you pilot a mech when we can barely keep our eyes open?'

'I might be a little sleepy now,' said Titch, 'but I'll be totally alert once I'm strapped inside that cockpit.'

'That's good news.' Martha sounded wary. She had just finished running the final system check on LoneStar. Now, like everyone else working in the Armoury, her attention was drawn to what sounded like the approach of some giant monster. 'It's time to say hello to your opponent for the final round.'

As she spoke, the ground beneath their feet began to shake. As the grinding and hissing of cogs and pistons grew louder, the crowds in the grandstands climbed to their feet in awe.

'It sounds big,' said Finn. 'Very big!'

Titch didn't disagree. A flock of seagulls took to the air from behind the warehouse overlooking the dock, while Championship stewards could be seen making sure that everyone was standing at a safe distance.

A moment later, the mech lumbered into view, to gasps from the other teams.

It was well over twice the size of any other machine in the Armoury, with glowing red eyes and steel horns sprouting from its forehead. The colossal metal beast possessed not just two arms but four, and each one gripped a different weapon — from a jagged buzzsaw, to a shotgun, a trap net, and the most formidable of all: a huge magnet. It was shaped like a club and crackled with electricity. As if to demonstrate its capabilities, the chrome beast levelled the magnet at a tugboat in the harbour. With a groan as the anchor tightened, and to gasps from all around, the vessel seemed to pop out of the water. It was too far away to see the rival pilot in the the cockpit. Even so, whoever was behind the controls clearly meant business. Just as the boat was about to connect with the magnetic club, the mech span around full circle and smashed it out towards the harbour wall.

'Is that really who we're fighting?' Titch paused to watch the vessel slam into the water out in the distance. He turned to Martha, who nodded glumly.

'Say hello to TitanAmok,' she said, only to grimace like her friends and turn her back on the din as the massive mech fired up the buzzsaw. 'OK, so now it's just showing off.'

'But how can this be allowed?' asked Finn. 'That mech has never fought a round in the Battle Championship. It can't just show up and fight!'

Titch thought back to the conversation he had overheard from the meeting of officials. It was time to tell Finn and Martha what he had witnessed.

'Some of the people around that table sounded very important,' he said to finish, having explained how he had sneaked into the building. 'I heard my dad protest but they wouldn't listen.'

The twins simply looked at one another in amazement when Titch revealed that he believed his father had been present.

'Didn't anyone else back him up?' asked Martha.

Titch looked to the ground for a moment.

'Marshal Johnson agreed it could put lives at risk.'

'What?' Finn looked stunned.

'The marshal is here as well?' asked Martha, clearly shocked. 'Why?'

Titch spread his hands and shrugged. At the same time, the enormous mech out on the dock roared at the crowd as if it were some giant ape that had just escaped from a hold. Titch grimaced at the din and then sighed.

'All I know is that right now we need to focus on this fight,' he told his two friends. 'And that's precisely what I intend to do in the next round, even if my opponent is here as a test of strength.'

Martha exhaled long and hard.

'Well, this weekend is becoming more mysterious by the moment,' she said, 'but you're right not to be intimidated. Titch, you've been top of the leaderboard throughout the season. This could be your chance to shine!'

For a moment, the three friends watched as the biggest mech they had ever seen destroyed another boat. They were so entranced that nobody noticed Alexei draw up alongside them.

'I wouldn't want to be in your cockpit seat,' he said, with his eyes locked on TitanAmok. 'Yesterday, I was gutted that I lost my battle round. Looking at who you've drawn to fight here, I think I've had a lucky escape!'

Titch ignored the comment, but remembered the wallet in his hand.

'This belongs to you,' he said,

explaining where he had got it from.

'Hey, thanks.' Alexei appeared genuinely surprised and also grateful. He looked up from the wallet and grinned. 'You know, you're not so bad after all. I still wouldn't want to be facing that beast today, but I guess I'll be rooting for you.'

Titch smiled and then shrugged.

'I appreciate your support,' he said. 'Let's face it, I can use as much as I can get!'

● ● ●

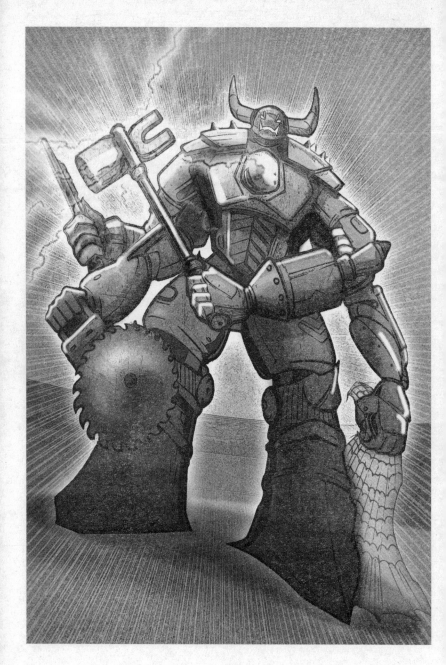

8
Clash of Power

'This fight could be messy,' said the onboard computer, as soon as Titch had strapped himself into the cockpit. 'I'll do my best to support you, but any hope of victory is going to take guts as much as quick wits.'

'I know that.' Titch fired up the monitoring system before checking his weapon status. For this third and final fight of the weekend, Martha had visited the Scavenger Store and returned with just one weapon. It didn't look like much, once she'd bolted it into LoneStar's grip, but she had assured Titch that one shot on target could finish his rival. Titch grasped the control stick and swung

LoneStar's firing arm in front of the hatch. With its flared muzzle, the weapon looked like an old-fashioned musket. It was the box of vintage switches, circuits, lights and switches strapped in front of the trigger that made Titch think it wasn't designed to fire plain old bullets. 'So, how does this work?' he asked.

'Under no circumstances must you fire it unless you're one hundred percent certain of hitting your target,' warned the onboard computer. 'It isn't called the EndGamer for nothing.'

'The EndGamer? You make it sound lethal!' Titch was smiling as he examined the weapon through the hatch, though in his heart he wondered if it could even dent his opponent. In his view, it looked a little homemade. Still, that didn't stop the crowd from going wild as Titch turned LoneStar to wave at them. 'Are you sure Martha hasn't been sold a dud?'

The onboard computer didn't respond for a moment. It was as if it wanted Titch to have a long, hard think about what he'd just said. 'The EndGamer is loaded with a miniature neutron bomb,' it reported finally. 'It's been carefully assembled to make it safe for the competition, but one strike will wipe out your opponent's mech.'

Titch nodded, but looked unconvinced.

'So, it's one weapon against four,' he said, just as the klaxon sounded to mark the beginning of the battle round. 'Where is TitanAmok?'

'The rules state that a mech can begin at any place on the battle ground,' said the onboard computer.

'But there's no sign of life on the monitor.'

As if in response, something exploded from the water out in the dock.

Titch spun LoneStar around just as his opponent rose up from the sea. The emergence of the machine caused great waves to roll out and wash over the wharves. The crowds shrieked in awe and delight as the spray peppered the ground in front of the grandstands.

'Now, that's what I call a surprise appearance,' said the onboard computer, but Titch wasn't listening.

'We need cover,' he cried, as he threw LoneStar into a sprint along the length of the dock. 'With the firepower that mech's packing, this battle round could be over in no time!!'

Sure enough, as LoneStar raced towards a stack of shipping containers, a series of missiles whizzed across their path. Each one smashed into the warehouse behind them, engulfing it in flames.

'Stay low, Titch!' warned the onboard computer, as another volley of missiles slammed into the building. 'This mech means business!'

Titch lunged for the cover of the containers. He threw LoneStar into a roll on hitting the ground and scanned the radar closely.

'It's advancing towards us,' he said out loud. 'Let's go live with the EndGamer.'

'You have just one chance,' the onboard computer reminded him.

It was the sound of the buzzsaw firing into life that seized Titch's attention next. He looked up and saw the blade bite through the containers in a shower of sparks. Directing LoneStar into a backwards scramble, Titch barely had time to grab his breath before his rival smashed through the wall. TitanAmok roared, swiping away several containers as if they were made from cardboard.

'There's only one thing for it,' muttered Titch, and lifted LoneStar onto its feet. 'Time to run!'

Titch had no intention of fleeing from

the battleground. What he needed was a chance to regroup and mount a counter-attack. Dodging several swipes from the buzzsaw, Titch threw LoneStar under the shadow of the giant machine and leaped into the water.

'What are you doing?' asked the onboard computer, who sounded shocked. 'We're not watertight, remember?'

'Getting wet is the least of our worries!' Titch yelled, as he focused on wading away from the dock. He glanced at the radar. The sea wall protected the harbour from the ocean swell, but it was the outcrop of jagged rock on the other side of the entrance that grabbed his attention. With a lighthouse mounted at the edge to prevent ships from being scuppered, Titch figured he could use it as cover as he prepared his counter-attack.

'That's where we need to be!' he yelled, as water began to seep through the lower section of the hatch. If I can draw TitanAmok into the water now, it'll give me a chance to target him with the EndGamer!'

Sure enough, on the radar Titch noted the large red circle following behind. LoneStar was moving as fast as he could push it, which wasn't easy in the water. Half the cockpit hatch was now submerged, which meant Titch could see the lighthouse ahead and the treacherous rocks underneath.

It was a view that came to an abrupt halt, however, when a fishing trawler barrelled right over LoneStar's head and smashed into the water in front of them.

'TitanAmok is putting his magnetic club to good use,' said the onboard computer, as the swell from the impact washed right over them. 'Watch out, Titch! Here comes another!'

Hauling LoneStar around, Titch was just in time to see the barge sailing through

the air towards them. He threw his mech sideways, narrowly avoiding the vessel as it crashed into the water. 'TitanAmok is way out of our league!' he cried. 'We can't compete against something like this. It doesn't belong in the Battle Championship!'

Fighting to keep LoneStar upright in the swell, Titch remembered what he had overheard in the official's meeting. TitanAmok had been designed to fight in wars, not competition! It also reminded him who had sounded the warning about sending a mech this menacing into the Championship battleground. His dad and Marshal Johnson!

'They were right,' he muttered, as he pushed on for the lighthouse. 'This is no longer a knockout round. It's a fight for survival!'

'Your father's been missing for years,' said the onboard computer. 'There is no recorded evidence that he's still alive.'

'I've seen him with my own eyes.' Titch prepared to clamber up the rocks to the lighthouse. 'Trust me, he's still with us!'

Another boat smashed into the water behind them as Titch steered LoneStar up the rocks. With no protection from the harbour wall, they were at the mercy of the sea. Waves crashed over the mech, threatening to wash them away. Titch could hear the roar of the crowd from the grandstands as well as from inmates on the prison island beyond the outcrop. Titch focused hard, well aware that his rival was closing in behind him – and fast. It was another volley of missile strikes that persuaded Titch to scramble over the last of the rocks.

'Luck must be on your side,' said the onboard computer. 'TitanAmok has yet to make a direct hit.'

'Then let's hope my luck doesn't run out!' Titch swung around to see his rival approaching the rocks. Behind him, the city skyscrapers dwarfed the docklands, and yet it looked as if every last citizen had gathered in the grandstands to witness this final round of the weekend. Titch had no time to consider just how many thousands were watching. Instead, watching TitanAmok wrench a boulder free, he sheltered LoneStar behind the lighthouse.

'The EndGamer is now locked and loaded,' confirmed the onboard computer as the boulder crashed to the ground beside them. 'Remember, Titch. One shot will decide whether you win or lose this round.'

'Winning or losing isn't so much of an issue right now,' said Titch, as the weapons screen went live. This showed a view from the cameras mounted in LoneStar's visor with a target sight at the centre. 'I just want to get out of here alive!'

Carefully, Titch directed LoneStar to peer around the lighthouse, only to see two chrome horns rise up on the screen. 'TitanAmok!' he gasped in surprise. He could do nothing but watch as the great mech grasped the lighthouse with both hands and headbutted it. The impact caused the structure to crack from top to bottom. With a single push from TitanAmok, Titch looked up to see an avalanche of bricks and dust plunging towards his mech.

• • •

9
End Game

Inside the cockpit, winded from the impact, Titch fired up the emergency lights. The reinforced glass hatch was cracked, but it had stopped the falling stonework from smashing through.

'Run a system check!' he ordered the onboard computer and grasped the controls. His mech was buried beneath tonnes of debris. He tried to move the machine, but it was trapped.

'We've taken some damage to the body shell,' reported the computer. 'Apart from the fact that we're buried right now, everything is functioning just fine.'

'Shh! What was that?' Titch strained to listen . . . and then he heard it again.

This time, the scraping sound was accompanied by a chink of light through the debris. 'TitanAmok is digging us out!' he cried.

'Somehow I don't think he's hoping to save us,' said the onboard computer.

'I'm not planning on waiting to find out!' said Titch.

With all his might, Titch pulled back on a control stick and then punched it forward. This time, the mech responded by smashing its fist upwards, through the mountain of bricks and into its rival's chest plate. TitanAmok rocked back with the impact and Titch was quick to follow it up with one slamming punch after another.

'You've taken him by surprise!' cried the onboard computer. 'Finish him, Titch!'

As TitanAmok staggered backwards, Titch hauled LoneStar onto its feet. Up close, his opponent dwarfed LoneStar, but Titch wasn't scared. Nor was he prepared to find his machine engulfed in the steel trap net that TitanAmok then fired at him. He tried to dodge away as the net opened wide, but it wrapped around the arm that brandished the EndGamer. Titch tried desperately to shake off the net, but that just made it all the more entangled. He turned to face TitanAmok, who had moved to higher ground. Titch prepared to pull the trigger, only for his opponent to strike first. With a scream, the missile slammed into LoneStar's shoulder. The impact rattled through the cockpit, knocking the mech into a spin.

'That was too close for comfort!' Titch yelled, over the blare of an emergency alarm.

'That arm is no longer functioning,' reported the onboard computer. 'Fortunately, your shooting arm suffered no damage. Unfortunately, it's still tangled in the net.'

'That's not good,' muttered Titch, moving LoneStar low across the ground as another missile screamed towards them. 'OK, I have an idea!'

Without further word, Titch threw his mech into the waves. Immediately, water began to spring through the hatch seal.

'Is this wise?' asked the onboard computer.

'What have we got to lose?' asked Titch. At the same time, he directed LoneStar to dive towards the sea bed. 'Has TitanAmok followed me yet?'

As if in response, a boulder plunged past the cockpit.

'Doesn't look like our opponent wants to get wet again,' said the onboard computer, as yet more rocks tumbled by. 'Titch, if we take on board much more water we'll never make it back onto dry land.'

'I just need a minute,' said Titch, pushing on towards the sea bed. As they went deeper, yet more cracks crossed the cockpit hatch, which caused him to gasp.

'It's the pressure,' said the onboard computer. 'We can't take much more!'

'Nearly there,' said Titch through gritted teeth, as the bed of the ocean took shape through the murk. 'And that's just what I came down here to find!'

Amid the seaweed and the fish lay several rusting shipwrecks. Titch had seen so many clogging the shallows he'd felt sure there would be more out here. Despite the fact that the cockpit was filling fast, he pushed LoneStar to the sea bed. There, he walked the mech towards the stern of a supertanker half buried in the silt and sand. Finally, Titch stopped in front of the sunken vessel's vast propeller. He lifted LoneStar's working arm, still tangled in the net, and used one of the blades to cut it free. It took a few attempts. When the net finally fell away, the water inside the cockpit had reached Titch's shoulders.

'We need to surface,' advised the onboard computer, sounding unusually tense. 'If we don't get away now we could be finished!'

'TitanAmok will be waiting for us if we rise up here! We'll be blown out of the water!'

Ignoring further protests from the computer, Titch turned LoneStar and swam around the base of the rocky outcrop. Finally, with the water so high inside the cockpit he could taste it, Titch steered the mech upwards. Breaking the surface, he was quick to clamber out onto the rocks. At once, the water in the cockpit began to drain away.

'That was close,' said the onboard computer.

'No,' said Titch, pushing LoneStar to the summit of the outcrop. 'This is close!'

Just ahead of them, TitanAmok was peering into the swell where LoneStar had first dived in. Back on the dock, the crowds in the grandstands went wild on seeing Titch's mech reappear. It left him with no time to hesitate. Taking aim with the EndGamer, freed now from the net, he found the trigger and prepared to fire. At the same time, drawn by the sudden roar from the crowd, TitanAmok looked up and then span around.

'Surprise!' Titch pressed the trigger, just as his rival fired back. It forced him to throw LoneStar to one side, narrowly avoiding several missiles that promptly raced across the surface of the ocean and slammed into the prison wall. Titch heard the explosion, but it was the blinding flash in front of him that commanded his attention as the EndGamer found its target. An intense heat accompanied the detonation. Titch quickly shielded his eyes. As the glare died away to a sound like thunder, he looked back to see a towering fireball. It rose up high in a column and then peeled away in rings.

Titch had never seen anything like it before. Nor did he feel that he wanted to witness such a thing again.

'Victory!' cried the onboard computer, as the fireball burned out and the smoke cleared in the sea breeze. The rocks were blackened where the machine once stood, but TitanAmok was nowhere to be seen. Titch eased LoneStar towards the crater where his rival had been standing – and that's when his attention locked on the swell behind the outcrop.

'There it is!' he cried, having spotted the machine face down in the water, scorched from head to toe and sparking from every joint. 'Can we reach the pilot on the radio? That was a massive blast!'

'The emergency channel is now open,' confirmed the onboard computer.

'This is Titch Darwin, LoneStar pilot,

do you read me? Are you in need of assistance? Talk to me!' Titch listened out, but heard only static.

'That mech is leaking fuel,' the onboard computer pointed out. 'Look how it's forming a slick!'

Titch brought LoneStar closer to the edge of the outcrop, only to recoil when a spark from the stricken mech ignited the fuel on the water. With a snapping sound, a blaze broke out across the harbour mouth, engulfing TitanAmok.

'I'm going in!' cried Titch, unbuckling his safety harness. 'We have to save the pilot!'

'Leave it to the fire marshals!' advised the onboard computer. 'They're on their way!'

Titch glanced across to the dock. Several launches with flashing lights had just set off towards them.

'There isn't time!' Titch climbed out of his seat, throwing open the cockpit hatch at the same time. As the last of the sea water fell away, the footplate slid out automatically, but Titch didn't wait for the steps to lock into position. Instead, he dived from the footplate, head first through the blaze and into the water.

It was freezing cold under the surface. Titch almost inhaled in shock, but kept his breath and swam underneath the hulking machine until he found the cockpit.

Through the glass, he could see a figure in flying goggles and a helmet

fighting to open the hatch. Titch found the manual release handle and pulled it hard. The hatch fell away. Sea water rushed into the cockpit, washing the figure into his arms. Desperate for air, Titch swam upwards with the pilot, heading away from the burning oil slick. At the surface, it was clear from the sirens that the rescue launches still had some way to go. By now, the blaze had spread and risen high into the air. Titch dragged the pilot onto the rocks. The pair rested on their hands and knees, coughing as they fought for breath.

'That was close!' said Titch.

He looked across at the pilot, who removed his helmet and then, with a sigh, lifted his goggles.

'Hello, son.'

● ● ●

10
In Flames

'Dad! I knew it!'

Titch recognised him straight away. He saw right through the huge scar on the side of his face. Without a doubt, this was the man who had disappeared on the Championship trail all those years ago. Titch blinked, in shock and surprise. His legs felt weak all of a sudden and his heart hammered hard. Dozens of questions sprang into his mind, but he couldn't find the words. Out in the harbour, some of the rescue launches were circling the blazing wreck of the mech, while others raced by in the direction of the prison island. There, as a result of TitanAmok's missile strike, a stream of convicts could be seen spilling out from a scorched hole in the jail wall, seizing the opportunity to escape.

Titch glanced back at his father. The man looked nervous.

'There's so much I have to tell you, Titch, but it isn't safe for either us right now. I have to go—'

'But you can't!' yelled Titch in desperation. 'I've been looking for you all this time. You can't disappear on me again!'

His father glanced warily at one of the launches as it approached the outcrop. 'There's more to this than meets the eye,' he said. 'The Battle Championship isn't just a sport. It's a secret military testing programme. Our nation is preparing for another global war, Titch. Only this time they plan to take the enemy by surprise and turn their lands to dust!'

'But what good will come from that?' asked Titch. 'The last war left the world in ruins. Why push for more destruction?'

His father shrugged, like the decision was out of his hands.

'Unfortunately for me,' he said, 'when I stumbled on the truth about the Battle Championship, the powers that be gave me a choice.'

'What was that?' Titch hung on every word his father uttered.

'Either work for them, developing new weapon systems in preparation for a surprise attack,' he said, and then sighed long and hard, 'or see my family suffer.'

Titch hung his head. 'I had no idea.'

A moment later, he felt his father's hand gently lift his chin.

'You just need to know that I love you, son,' he told him. 'I never meant to vanish. I just had to put your safety first.'

'But you just put me through the toughest battle round of my life!' said Titch, finding his voice now. 'How could you?'

'To protect you,' his father said. 'When I found out that they were planning on testing out TitanAmok in the battle round, I had to volunteer to be the pilot. Any other pilot would've crushed LoneStar. You could've been seriously hurt!'

'Did you throw the lob bomb with the message through my window?' Titch asked. 'Was it you who wanted me to pack up for the weekend?'

His father nodded solemnly.

'I just wanted to keep you safe from

harm,' he confessed. 'I put on a show of strength to satisfy the powers that be, but I didn't expect you to win the round, Titch! That took guts, as did swimming out there just now and rescuing me. I owe you my life!'

Titch could still barely believe that his father was here and talking to him. He also couldn't understand why he was looking so edgy when the rescue crew on the launch reached the outcrop.

'Stay,' he pleaded. 'We can work it out

together.'

'I have to go before I'm recognised,' he said. 'If my handlers find out that we've spoken, they'll punish you and the family back home!'

'What handlers?' asked Titch. 'It sounds like this programme needs exposing before there's another war!'

'If the enemy find out, they'll be sure to strike first,' said his father. 'Far better that I find a way to put a stop to it from the inside. Marshal Johnson is working closely with me to find a way. They dragged him into this years ago, threatening his family in the same way they threatened mine. Now we can only seek to call a halt to this programme if you stay quiet!'

Titch watched his father rise to his feet, aware that members of the crew were on the rocks below them.

'Please don't go,' said the boy as hot tears filled his eyes.

'You put on one heck of a fight, boy,' he said, and grasped Titch by the shoulders. 'I'll remember this moment. Always.'

As the rescue personnel turned their attention towards them, Titch's father looked one way and then the other before taking off along the outcrop. Titch watched him clamber over the rocks, heading for the docks and beyond. He only glanced away when a crew member from the rescue launch called up to ask if he was injured. When he looked back, his father was gone.

'Doesn't look like Daddy wants to stick around.'

Titch spun around to see a familiar figure at the end of the outcrop. Wyatt Thorne was leaning against LoneStar, using a matchstick to pick at his teeth. Behind him, on the prison island, a fire had broken out amid the chaos. Some convicts had hijacked rescue launches to get away, while others were swimming for land. The outlaw glanced over his shoulder and grinned. 'Seems like everyone is in a big hurry to leave, but not me. I figured it was worth stopping by just to see the look on your face.'

Titch felt a surge of anger rising inside him.

'You can't torment me any more!' he told Wyatt, bristling visibly. 'I've seen my father with my own eyes. At least I know that he's alive and looking out for me!'

By now, a full-scale emergency operation was taking shape out in the water. Along with the fire boats, pumping water onto the blazing fuel fire, several police vessels could be seen speeding towards the prison island.

Wyatt chuckled to himself.

'That jail held some of the most notorious mech smugglers in the country,' he crowed. 'Looks like trouble ahead for the Battle Championship!'

'We'll see about that,' said Titch. He was still reeling from coming face to face with his father – and desperately sad that he had gone. Still, deep inside, he knew he had to trust his dad, and that meant preparing for the next Championship season knowing that someone close to his heart was watching over him. And when the time came to call a halt to this secret operation going on behind the scenes, he would be ready to stand by his father. Nobody would stop him. Certainly not Wyatt Thorne, who seemed to enjoy seeing Titch look so torn by his father's brief return.

'Enjoy your freedom,' Titch told the bandit, and gestured at a police boat now speeding towards the outcrop. 'It won't last long.'

Then, hearing voices behind him, Titch turned to see Martha and Finn picking their way across the rocks. Marshal Johnson was with them. Seeing him, Wyatt

Thorne chuckled to himself.

'I don't suppose these kids expected to find you here either,' he called across to the marshal.

'I'm on official business,' replied Johnson, drawing the twins to his side. He looked across at Titch, nodding as if he was aware of the conversation that had just taken place between the boy and his father. 'As I've just explained to Finn and Martha, it's also classified business.'

Wyatt pretended to look impressed.

'Seems like lot of secrets have been swilling around this weekend,' he said, with a glance at the inferno that still consumed the mech out in the harbour entrance.

'Do you want us to fetch the sheriff?' asked Finn.

'Just say the word,' Martha added.

'Too late,' said the outlaw. 'You'll have to try harder if you want to catch me!' As he spoke, a motor launch pulled up beside

the outcrop behind him. Titch recognised several unshaven faces on board. These guys were part of Wyatt's gang, the Wired Bunch. They seemed very pleased to have their boss back on board.

'Keep your eyes peeled, Titch,' said Wyatt, as the pilot of the launch gunned the engine. 'Next time you hit the Championship trail, we'll be lying in wait.'

As the bandit's launch sped away, Titch turned his attention to the battered mech that had brought him this far. LoneStar looked in desperate need of repair. Even so, Titch knew the onboard computer was tuned into events because the cockpit lights began blinking brightly.

'As a team, we'll take on anyone who stands in our way,' he declared, as Martha, Finn and Marshal Johnson picked their way across the rocks to join him. 'This might be our first Battle Championship season, but the real fight has only just begun!'